Adventures of Coup & Friends

Susan McKallor

LifeRich Publishing is a registered trademark of The Reader's Digest Association, Inc.

LifeRich Publishing books may be ordered through booksellers or by contacting:

LifeRich Publishing
1663 Liberty Drive
Bloomington, IN 47403
www.liferichpublishing.com
1 (888) 238-8637

Because of the dynamic nature of the Internet, any web addresses or links contained in this book may have changed since publication and may no longer be valid. The views expressed in this work are solely those of the author and do not necessarily reflect the views of the publisher, and the publisher hereby disclaims any responsibility for them.

Any people depicted in stock imagery provided by Thinkstock are models, and such images are being used for illustrative purposes only. Certain stock imagery © Thinkstock.

ISBN: 978-1-4897-0835-9 (sc)
ISBN: 978-1-4897-0836-6 (e)

Print information available on the last page.

LifeRich Publishing rev. date: 8/11/2016

These stories are dedicated to Nancy Craun, a very dear friend and mentor. Without her encouragement and support over the years, these stories would have never come to life.

Endorsement by Susan Moger, college writing instructor, Anne Arundel Community College

"This collection of stories is a portrait of a loving friendship between Coup, an endearing stuffed dog, and Susie, his sensible friend. Their shared adventures—some suspenseful, some funny, all inspiring—include many expressions of the strong faith that bolsters Coup and Susie. The stories, told in Coup's distinctive voice, will appeal to anyone who has ever loved a stuffed dog to life."

Contents

Acknowledgments

Many thanks to Debbie Devine, the illustrator, for her patience and guidance and for her awesome artwork, which helped me bring Coup to life. It has been a pleasure working with her.

A special thank-you to Janice Hamilton, author and editor, for all her time reviewing and formatting my manuscript for submission. Without her, I don't know what I would have done.

Thanks to all my countless friends and family members for their time and patience while listening to Coup's stories.

Lastly, thanks to the staff at LifeRich Publishing for fielding all my questions and guiding me through the editing and publishing process.

Prologue

Have you ever met a talking stuffed dog who sounds like someone's best friend? I would like you to meet me! Coup is my name. I am an adorable stuffed dog. I become real to everyone I meet. I will inspire you, entertain you, and steal your heart!

Meet Coup with a C

I have mystical powers that allow me to look inside your heart and help to heal whatever may be bothering you. My listening abilities are enhanced by my very large and floppy ears. I have a gift that allows me to help turn every negative situation into a more positive one. Together, you and I will learn how to pray and ask God for help. Most importantly, we will always give thanks to God after He has guided us through all the rocky storms that may occur in our lives.

Now for my appearance: I have orange-yellowish fur that's beginning to wear, especially on the top of my head. I cover it nicely with a sporty blue baseball cap. I take great pride in my appearance. I am a very charming and warm-hearted companion, very easy to love. You and I will become close buddies in no time at all.

How Coup Met Susie

Crammed into a very small cardboard box with clear plastic on the front, bright lights half-blinding me, I tried over and over to open the lid at the top of the box. My front paws just did not seem to stretch far enough for me to get the lid open. Ooh, before I go any further, let me introduce myself. My name is Coup. With my paws stretched over my head, I am approximately thirteen inches tall. I am covered with orange-yellowish fur, and I have a big black nose and two really large black eyes.

I am standing on a shelf in a drugstore with other assorted toys. I am the only dog. I cannot get this box to open up and allow me to move about, so I must try another tactic. I will say a little prayer to God. "Find a way to free me from this box, please! And place me in the arms of someone who will love me."

Shortly after my prayer, the miracles began to happen. This young lady came over to the toys. She looked at several different items, and at first she walked right past me and smiled. Her smile made me feel all warm inside, but she walked right past my box and out of the store.

The next day I decided I had to draw more attention to myself. I tried rocking the box back and forth, but I wasn't very successful with that action. So I tried a little more force—oops! All of a sudden, before I could do anything, the box fell off the shelf onto the floor. I went from a standing position to being all crumpled up in one corner of the box, which was lying on the floor.

Then I realized someone had lifted me from the floor and was holding my box up in the air. I looked up to see the lady from the day before, and she was now holding my box. She gave me one of those great big smiles, and my heart lit up! I felt special. I learned that her original plan was to purchase me as a gift for some little boy named David, but fate intervened, and that union never occurred. Susie wanted me for herself. On that special day, she spoke to me and called me by name. She said, "Well, Coup, I think you may be going home with me. My name is Susie, and I have been looking all over for a dog just like you. I have a special place for you in my home."

Susie and I headed to the checkout line so she could pay for me. I was so happy that I just could not stay still. Susie told me, "You must calm down," while she was driving the car.

Susie took the big box and laid it down on the front seat of the car. She set me on top of it. It was great! I could see out the window! Oh, I was just so excited! My mind was racing with thoughts. Where were we going? What would her house look like? Where would she place me in her home? Would I meet other stuffed friends?

Soon we pulled into a driveway. Susie parked her car and gently lifted me up from the big, old, ugly box. She would eventually throw away that box that had held me captive for so many years. We headed down a long hallway with doors on either side. I wondered, Which door leads to my room? At the very end of the hall, Susie opened a door, and we walked into a beautiful bedroom. There was a large window lit brightly by the glowing sun. There were green plants sitting on white wicker stands. Then I saw it: a magnificent bed with a lovely flowered bedspread, soft pink, and big pillows—lots and lots of pillows. I just wanted to run and jump on the pillows to see if they were as soft as they appeared.

Susie placed me on top of the floral bedspread and gently laid my head up against a very soft pillow. Oh, it just felt so good to relax and lie back against the softness of this pillow. "Oh, my gosh!" I exclaimed. The good Lord had answered another of my prayers. He had found someone very special to love me and take wonderful care of me. "Dear Lord, thank you so much for the wonderful blessings, lessons, and gifts. Amen!"

One of the Family

Susie sat me down on the overstuffed chair in the living room after our long day at the beach. I was just trying to catch my breath. Then, all of a sudden, up jumps Gibbers, Susie's real, live dog. As he sat next to me, he scooted up really close so I could lean against him.

Gibbers was an old dog with beautiful, long, multicolored fur. He was very affectionate to me. He welcomed me into Susie's home right from the first day. Gibbers accepted me as if I were one of his own pups. He loved to groom me when we spent time together.

When he first started licking my face and coat, I thought, "Yuck! What is this dog doing to me?" Maybe something had spilled onto my fur and he was licking

it off? Then Susie explained that Gibbers was just licking my fur to groom me, as he would do with one of his own pups.

So I just learned to accept the practice of grooming from Gibbers. He was one of my best friends at Susie's house. He not only groomed me; he protected me from that mean old cat, Albert, who was also part of the household.

The only problem with his licking was that it made my fur all damp and sticky. It would take hours for my fur to dry. Not wanting to insult Gibbers, my old friend, I just kept praying and asking God to help Gibbers find a new friend he could groom.

Over the Edge

I awoke, not realizing where I was or what had happened to me. All I knew for sure was that my big nose hurt. As I opened one eye, then the other, it seemed as though my face was very close to something. I sniffed at it, trying to figure out what it was. Sniffing didn't reveal any clues. I tried to move my front and back paws, but they were all stuck underneath my body. I kept thinking, "What has happened to me? Where am I? Where is Susie?" Finally I began to pray, as I often do when I get into a situation where I need some help. I said, "Dear Lord, help me figure all this out, and bring Susie to my rescue."

Finally, as I was moving about, I realized I was face down on the carpet. I slowly turned my head and realized I was up against the side of the big recliner chair. Susie usually places me on the edge of the big recliner's arm when she sits down to read. But there have been many times when Susie will sit down and pop right back up when she remembers that she has forgotten something or when the phone rings.

On this particular occasion, the phone rang. Susie popped up out of the chair. I fell over the edge of the armchair. Down I went, face first, smashing my large nose on the carpet. The fall must have knocked me out for a minute or two. When I awoke, I was dazed and unsure of my whereabouts.

But as soon as Susie finished her call and sat back down, she noticed her old pal was no longer sitting in his favorite spot on the edge of the armchair. Susie looked over the edge to find me rubbing my sore nose. She reached down and scooped me up in her arms and gave me a great big belly hug. I silently thanked God for answering my prayers.

Susie's Kitchen

Ah, what is that smell from Susie's kitchen? It could be anything from crispy fried chicken to corn fritters. On this particular afternoon, I came downstairs to find Susie whipping up one of her famous dark molasses cakes. Yum!

I climbed up onto one of the kitchen chairs so I could get a better look. I stood by Susie to see what she was doing. She had set out on the table a large array of ingredients for this luscious cake. There was a small, funny-shaped bottle of vanilla extract, some baking soda and baking powder, big bags of flour and powdered sugar, butter, two eggs, milk, and a bottle of molasses. I also saw a dish of softened butter and two round cake pans. Susie had placed a large bowl on the table, and she asked me to fetch her the flour sifter. I jumped over the cabinets where Susie kept all her baking items and finally found the sifter. I asked Susie if I could do the sifting for her. She was a little hesitant at first. Finally, after all my pleading, she agreed. Excited, I poured the premeasured flour and other dry items into the sifter and began sifting and shaking it to get every last ounce into the bowl. What I didn't notice was that I was not close enough to the bowl, so quite a bit of the flour had missed the bowl and spilled onto the floor. I got down on the floor and under the table to try to collect the spilled flour. Next, while trying to get back up to my original position at the table, I was slipping and sliding all over the kitchen floor. I had flour all over me—on my hind paws and face. Finally I just sat on the flour as Susie glared at me and shouted, "What a mess! Dog, what are you doing? Pay more attention and get closer to the bowl when you are sifting, and get off the floor!"

Susie finished up the cake by adding all the remaining ingredients. As she was pouring the batter into the cake pans, I asked if I could lick the bowl. She said, "You can have a spatula full, and that's it." She wanted me out of the kitchen. I had done enough damage for one day.

I sat in the living room and tried to kill time until the cake was out of the oven. I played and ran after my ball for a while. Pretty soon I heard the oven timer ring.

"Yippee! It is finally time to get the cake out and begin the frosting!"

Susie told me, "Be careful playing around the oven door while it is open. You could get burned."

Ouch! I thought. Susie set the hot cake pans down on a wooden board. She told me that I would have to wait a few more minutes while the cakes cooled. Meanwhile Susie mixed up some molasses, sugar, vanilla, and a little butter for the frosting. I asked Susie, "Where is your recipe for this cake? I want to read it and see just what is in it."

Susie replied, "There isn't any recipe. I just put in a little of this and a little of that, and God does the rest, and before you know it, we have another delicious cake to enjoy. It isn't hard to do."

The cake had finally cooled enough to take it out of the tins. Each cake came out beautiful, all round and perfect. Susie frosted the cake. The cake was still a little warm, so the frosting began to run down the sides, dripping onto the plate. I ran my paw up the sides of the cake and licked the frosting off as soon as it trickled down. I got the frosting from paw to mouth without Susie noticing. Then, all of a sudden, I moved closer to the cake so I could get a paw full of frosting—but I slipped, landing face first on the cake.

Susie picked me up by the seat of my pants and shook her head. "You just can't seem to stay out of trouble," she said. She wiped me off, set me on the chair next to the table, and told me to stay put as she went over to the sink and started washing the dirty dishes. After finishing the dishes, Susie took her spatula and further smoothed the icing over the cake. Then it looked a lot more presentable. She then told me I could not have a piece of cake until after lunch. As always, it was difficult to wait that long, but I managed.

"Oh, boy, this is yummy!" I said as I licked off the frosting on my front paw. It was well worth the wait.

I thanked Susie for allowing me to help her make the cake and told her how delicious it was. I look forward to my next adventure in Susie's kitchen.

A Fur-Job

After many years of wear and tear, I made the biggest decision of my life: to undergo a fur-job. Susie knew a lady who did a lot of sewing. The lady had offered to look at me and see if she could repair my old fur.

One afternoon Susie made arrangements for us to meet with Maureen so she could take a look at my ragged fur. I was terrified that this lady would be rough with me and would not be as patient as Susie. Susie and I arrived at this beautiful old home nestled back in the woods. It had a long pathway that led up to the front door. As we got closer to the door, I could hear loud barking. Immediately I was on my guard about what was on the other side of that door. But as the door slowly opened, I saw an attractive older lady with snow-white hair and a warm smile, and beside her stood a huge lab, who was wagging his tail. I thought, "So far, so good." The dog seemed quite friendly.

Immediately Maureen reached out and took me from Susie's arms. She held me up, examined my fur closely, and said, "Well, young fella, you and I have a big job on our hands."

I thought, *Well, it sounds like she is willing to work with me and give this thing a try.* Later Susie, Maureen, and I discussed the game plan. It would take four to five days to repair most of my fur completely. That meant I had to remain with Maureen during the entire period. Susie and Maureen continued to chat. I was thinking to myself, *I don't want to stay here with a complete stranger! What am I going to do?*

Susie stood up to leave. She picked me up and gave me a great big belly hug. She told me that I would be just fine for those four or five days and that she would call and check on me frequently. After we had said our good-byes, Maureen took me into her sewing room. I was surprised to see how bright and cheery the room was, lit by the sun shining through the windows!

Later that day, Maureen took me and laid me down on a big table where some beautiful, thick, furry fabric was stretched out. The table seemed really hard at first. After a while, though, my little body got used to it. Maureen picked up a huge pair of scissors to cut out the fabric she had just traced and outlined around me. I was shaking by then, fearing Maureen would either drop the scissors on me or cut my little paws with it. But Maureen was very gentle. She was careful with the scissors, and she spoke to me in a very soothing way. She could see me shaking as I lay quietly on the fur.

Next I noticed this object that looked like a big tomato. When Maureen picked it up, I realized the tomato was filled with tiny pins.

Oh, no! I thought. *She's not going to touch me with that.* Then Maureen picked up the pincushion and plucked a pin from it. I held my breath, asking God, *Please do not let this woman stick me with those pins.* Maureen gently placed the pins in the fabric around my foot, not in me. Finally I could relax for a moment.

Every day Maureen would come into the sewing room. There she had placed me on soft pillows in a big chair. She would pick me up and ask me, "How's my buddy feeling today?" This interaction really made me feel special. Each day

Maureen came closer to completing the work on my tattered little body. I began to look more and more like a new dog rather than the tattered dog that I had been before I arrived. My fur-job was starting to pay off.

Finally all the work was complete. Susie was called to fetch her trusty pal. I could hardly wait to see Susie and show off my new fur-job. Suddenly there was a knock at the door.

"Yay! It is Susie!" I shouted. She had returned to reclaim me.

I was so happy! I was afraid I might split one of my new seams. Susie could not believe how brave her little buddy had been to sit so still for hours while Maureen rebuilt most of his fur. My fur was fresh and new up to my chin. Susie asked Maureen why she had stopped there.

Maureen said, "I felt it would take away from Coup's personality to replace the fur on his face and snout." So she had just left my face as it was and told me I would have to buy myself a snappy ball cap to hide my balding head. I felt like a pup again with all the new fur.

"And just think," I told myself, "with all the extra fur, I will be able to stay much warmer this winter."

Strutting my new fur-job and ball cap, I was a show-off at Susie's place.

Challenged by Fear

On several pillows on Susie's bed, with more pillows on both sides, I felt as though I was in heaven. I gradually inched over, closer to Susie. I wanted to be right up underneath her arm so I could feel the warmth of her body next to mine.

On this Sunday, Susie wasn't feeling her best and seemed listless and distant. She and I just weren't communicating much. Deep down inside, I knew she must be seriously ill. I tried to keep quiet so I would not disturb her. I was frightened that someone would take her away, and I'd be left behind to face all my greatest fears. My greatest fears were that something would happen to Susie and that Susie would not return home.

Then I had to face my first great fear. I found myself riding on the edge of a stretcher going down a cold hospital hallway. There were lots of people scurrying about. I looked up at Susie, and her face was so pale.

I felt so helpless. I could not reach her or touch her or even feel her close to me. I could only watch her face. Finally we arrived at a room with a bed with all the covers turned down. Susie was moved over onto the bed, and finally someone picked me up and placed me next to Susie's head. I was so relieved to be much closer to Susie and to be able to touch her face. I whispered in her ear, "Are you okay?" There was no reply.

I thought that I would just try again in a few moments. Hours passed, and I scooted a little closer to Susie and whispered in her ear again. Still no reply! Then I was really worried. When Susie did not respond to me or help to make me talk, I knew she was really feeling poorly, as she was on this day. As I sat there on Susie's bed, I began to pray and ask God to please restore my special friend to good health. As the tears ran down my old furry face, I was so frightened I might lose her. Several days passed, and there were no sounds from my best friend's lips. Finally, one evening, Susie stirred a little, and then I felt her reach over and pick me up to take me in her arms. She gave me a great big belly hug and told me how much she loved me. Ah, I was so relieved to know my old friend was going to be okay! I looked into her eyes and saw the huge smile on her face.

While I waited for Susie to stir, I knew, deep within my heart and soul, that God was sitting there with Susie and me. But doubt entered my spirit, and it became difficult to believe God was actually there. But a few short prayers got rid of all the doubt and made all the difference in the world.

Lost Sock

The bedroom is quiet, but many sounds come up from downstairs. There Susie is working in the kitchen. I smell the dry, dusty heat as it rises from the floor register. I believe I hear the coffee machine sputtering out its last few drops. Susie seems to be gathering items from within the refrigerator—some deviled eggs, stinky old things. I do not know how anyone can enjoy eating deviled eggs. I also hear water running from the sink downstairs as Susie washes up her dishes.

In my bedroom at the top of the stairs, I examine my colorful selection of clothing. Yes, I believe I have one of each bright color to wear. My tie-dyed shirt is made of a very lightweight fabric—summer attire, I realize, but it is so pretty! The black cargo pants have a heavier feel. They will be just right for the cold and blustery weather today—I can hear the wind picking up a little outside now. *Brrr!* I shiver in my skimpy tee shirt. I dig through my closet for something that is bright and also warm to wear on my chilly arms. Ah, I find just the thing, a bright orange hoodie. This will work just fine! Now I feel a bit warmer.

But where is my yellow wool spaceship sock? I managed to put one sock on before misplacing the other one. I look again in my dresser drawer, then on and under the bed, and lastly in my closet—even though I never put my socks there unless they are dirty. The sock was just nowhere to be found! I feel stumped. I take a moment to say a little prayer and ask God to help me locate my yellow spaceship sock.

I could hear Susie coming up the stairs. "She'll be able to find the sock for me. She is really good at finding things." Susie enters my room. She can see my puzzled look.

"What's up?" Susie asks.

I say, "I just cannot seem to locate my other bright yellow sock."

Susie says, "Are you sure you have checked everywhere?"

"Yeah!" I reply.

Susie smiles and says, "I will give you a hint. Try looking at your right paw." I bend down and look at my right paw. Sure enough, there is my sock, tightly grasped in my paw, ready to put on!

Well, I thought, *God has come through for me again, and just in the nick of time.*

Susie says, "Go ahead and finish getting your clothes on so we will not be late for Cleveland's birthday party."

"Thank you, God, for all your help today! Amen!"

Bright Colors

laying around, having fun sliding down the banister, I feel so excited because my friend Cleveland has invited me to his birthday party. Susie is coming along. I yell downstairs to Susie, "What should I wear? I want to wear some of my Christmas clothes." (I had received a pink, purple, and yellow tie-dyed tee shirt, bright yellow socks with spaceships on them, and a neon pink ball cap.) I think, I will put on my gray and green camouflage pants. That should do it.

Susie suggested to me, "Pick one or two of your favorite outfits to wear and exchange your camouflage pants for the black cargo pants."

But I insisted I wanted to wear all my new, bright colors. "My black pants are so boring," I complained. "I need something to jazz my outfit up a little, something with lots of bright colors."

Susie said, "Oh, my goodness! You will be the laughingstock of the party." Generally I take great pride in what I put on, but this time Susie thought I had gone a little overboard. Susie sat down on the window seat and gazed out over the snowy path. Her thoughts were a million miles away; perhaps she was imagining the reactions of her doggy's friends as he entered the party. Off in the distance, she could hear her name called and feel someone tugging at her hand. It was Coup. He had changed his mind and taken her advice to wear the black cargo pants. Susie came out of her trance to see her best friend, pretty dapper, standing before her. Susie told me how sharp I looked and what a great job I had done with my selection. I just beamed from ear to ear. Susie told me to have a seat in the living room while she changed

her clothes. I wandered into the kitchen to grab some biscuits to jam into my pockets for the long ride to Cleveland's house.

After I filled my pockets, I thought I would find a place to hide on the front porch. I wanted to see if Susie could find me. Time passed, and there was no sign of Susie.

What is she doing? I thought. I was freezing on the porch. I looked for another place to hide, somewhere out of the bitterly cold wind. I am not sure just how long I was out there, but I needed my jacket badly.

Wandering all over the house, Susie was looking for me. "Just where did he get off to?" she said. As she walked downstairs, Susie shouted, "Coup! Where are you? We need to leave! Coup! I'm not kidding! If you are hiding, come out this minute!" Susie walked to the window and peered out. Next to the big pillar was a trembling little dog dressed in a bright tee shirt and black cargo pants. Susie rushed out the front door and wrapped her half-frozen friend in her arms. I trembled, so relieved to be taken back into the warmth of our home.

Well, needless to say, I never made it to my friend's birthday party so I could show off my bright colors. Chilled through my stuffing, I was in no condition to go anywhere. Susie took me back upstairs to bed, where I remained for the next couple of days. Cleveland and a few of my other friends dropped by to encourage me to feel better and to let me know I had been truly missed at the party. Cleveland told me, "The party just wasn't the same without you there!"

While I was resting in my bed, I did a lot of thinking. Next time I'm invited to a birthday party, I will try not to get into any mischief beforehand. I really hated missing Cleveland's party.

Dear Lord, Please remind me when I'm invited to a party to not get into trouble beforehand. Thanks, Lord. Oh, one last thing, Lord, please guide me as I encourage readers to watch for my next book, *Kooper with a "K"-- My Big Brother."*